Heart Hacker

FanatiXx Publication
ISO 9001:2015 CERTIFIED

FanatiXx Publication
AM/56, Basanti Colony, Rourkela 769012, Odisha
ISO 9001:2015 CERTIFIED
Website: *www.fanatixx.in*

"Heart Hacker"

By: Naaznin Mohamed

ISBN: 978-93-89923-54-4

Collection of English Quotes 1st Edition

Book Formatting: Saizal Gupta

Cover Design: Sagar Samal

Disclaimer

This is a work of fiction. Names, characters, places, and incidents are either the product of author's imagination or have been used illustratively and any resemblance to any person, living or dead, events or locales is entirely coincidental.

Naaznin Mohamed asserts all rights to be identified as the author of this work.

Acknowledgement

Everyone is having a Super Hero in our Life, without him we can't be here, yeah, I'm telling about my Real hero in my Life. Yup, He is my Dad.

I'm eternally grateful to "my Life" (My Dad) and I want to thank everyone, those who are supporting me to write a lot, and I love to thank my Soul sister Thasnim Fathima and My Besties Preethi, Venisha.

And Thanks to Everyone on my Publishing Team of FanatiXx Publication.

My Ever-patient publishing Manager Akshat Lakhe and Saizal Gupta.

And my First and Foremost Special thanks to my Readers, because you only giving a Soul to my Book by Reading it All Glories to be God

About the Author

Welcome to my Wonderful World, I'm Naaznin 21 years old girl who is pursuing electronics Communication Engineering, And In my life, Writing plays a vital Role, Writing is not just My Hobby, It's my Passion. Writing is a Self Help and Stress Buster to me.

Words has a super power to Heal you and Peel you, So Use it Carefully. Are you Ready? I'm gonna Hack your Heart, that's why I named the Book as "Heart Hacker", It's a Wonderful Communication which is going to happen Between your Heart and My words, So, keep Smiling and Reading.

The Motto of the Book is to Reveal the Power of Positivity and Creativity, Wait I'm not an adviser, I'm a Writer. And Always say in your Bad times," This shall too Pass". And I inspired from the Iron Lady of Pakistan,"Muniba Mazari".

I want to dedicate this Book to My "Dad".

Contents

1.Root of Relation

It's very easy to lose
Others trust, but its
Very hard to *gain* others *trust*.

2.Common Mistake

Don't break your own
Strong heart by telling it,
That you're weak.

3.Wife Become your Life

Hey man, why worry?
Life brings *wife* as your
Unconditional *love*, so
Keep *work* hard.

4. Buy Happiness

Buy an unlimited happiness
By *helping* the poor people,
It eliminates your worries,
And adds a *huge happiness.*

5. Learn to Accept

Do you know?
Life is getting *better,*
When you start *accepting*
And stop expecting.

6. Infinite Love

You can't count the *stars,*
So, your *love* and care on others
Should be like a *star.*

7.Best Motivator

The *motivator* for you
In the world is the
Only *you*.

8.Love is Back

You can bring back
Your *love* by
loving and caring *others*.

9.Jealous Kills

Learn to *live* without jealous,
And see that
How your life will become *fabulous*.

10. Love to take Risk

You can't lead
A *good* life without
Overcome from your *comfort* zone.

11. See the Good in Bad

Light may *spark*,
But it can't *spark* without
The dark.

12. Hacker of Heart

Love does not come
from luck,
It's not comes by trick
But by *heart hack*.

13. True LimeRack

Repeated lies never be a fact,
Your every action should create an impact,
Life is simple,
When you've the ability to *understand* the people,
Then mind it, your every good deeds and bad deeds will
always reflect.

14. Who's Gonna be with you?

Some people like a
Passing clouds,
But rare people only
Stay in your life like a *sky*.

15. Life Lessons

Don't search for a *best* tutor
To learn some best *lessons*,
Because, life is more than enough.

16. Who is Wrong?

Don't force anyone to agree
Your points,
If you force them means,
You're *unstable* with your words.

17. Heaven in your Home

Turn off the air cooler,
Let's go and sleep at the terrace
Feel the chillness of nature's wind
And *wake up* with fresh mind.

18. Solution for All Problems

Before you judge someone,
Just think, *imagine* and
Stand in their *situation*.

19. Magic of Music

Music produces in the air,
It can *boost* you up from the despair.

20. Know your Uniqueness

Never compare yourself with others,
Everyone is *unique* in their own way,
So, you're the *best*.

21. Smile Heals

Your *smiling* is also a charity,
It reveals your character's quality.

22.Nature is Our Future

There is no green without rain,
There is no *gain* without pain,
There is no coin without the sides of twin.

23.Secret of Soulmate

You can't live a life
Without any checkmate,
But you can escape from it,
When you're having a right wife
To protect you as your *soulmate*.

24.Let's Make History Together

The story never ends,
Until your life changes into *history*,
That undefeatable *history*,
Which can make a victory.

25.Shield of World

Green is the colour of pleasance,
The green which envelops
Our entire world,
And protect like a *shield*.

26.Help the Needy

Show your *mercy* to the needy
Through your currency.

27.Claim it Soon

There is no way without destiny,
There is no life without aim,
So, you've to *claim*.

28. Lack of Time

When you want to talk with them,
They're busy,
When they want to talk with you,
You're busy,
Then life becomes an *uneasy*.

29. Shyness Shines

When you hide in the clouds,
I can see your shyness
Which brings coolness,
That moment, I'm in *happiness*.

30. Be Aware of Fake Trust

Do not *deceive* others
By giving a fake love
And fake trust.

31.Play the Patience

Time passes like passing clouds,
But how we're standing with a *patience*
Like a sky is matters.

32.Priceless Memory

Poetry may not give any salary,
But it gives a lot than salary,
As *precious* memory.

33.Dream your Aim

Let's open up your *confidence*,
And close your fear tightly
With aim.

34.Knows your Individuality

Try to accept the *reality*,
Coz,it only reveals your individuality.

35.Be Calm and become Fame

Don't be rough to others, while
They curse you,
But be like a deaf to others,
While they curse you,
And *prove* yourself who you are?

36.Won ?

"Now" is the reflection
Of "won", so
Don't wait, do it
Right now.

37. Precious Moments

Eyes wears tears to "forget" the pain,
Lips wears smile to "forgive" the pain,
But when tears and smiles join together,
That pain becomes gain
Until, wait for that moment.

38. Carve your Identity

Negativity destroys your creativity,
Positivity creates your *identity*.

39. Three Letter Poison

It's already late,
So, *go* and talk with your loved one
Without any "ego",
Coz they are not a someone,
They're your favourite one.

40.Map your Dream

Life doesn't give you a chance only,
It gives a map and guide you
To *reach* your destiny.

41.Bitter Become Butter

Bitter butter is always better
Then the sweetest poison,
Never prefer the *fake* happiness.

42.Open your Heart

I love surprising *gifts*
To get,
Yeah, I love my *life*.

43. Secret of Love

You can't have
A *true* love,
Until you are true to them.

44. Who is Fool?

Once you get caught
With your *parental love,*
You can't fool them or cheat them.

45. Not an Advice

Don't trust anyone *blindly,*
Coz they can make you blind,
Without any kind.

46. Dream of Future

Roaming with *nature*
Is my big dream
In the *future*.

47. Alert

If you can't control your *anger*
Then, you can't protect your life
From the *danger*.

48. Wanted True Love

Nowadays break ups are *fashion*,
And patch ups are *passion*,
First one week, he has a *crush* on one girl,
After few weeks, he has a *crash* with that girl,
Relationship becomes single is a casual one on *Facebook*,
They change their life partner like a wear coz of *Outlook*,
So, taken may taken,
All are having a *love*,
My question is,
Is it true?
How long will you love them?

49. Name of the Movie

Now I'm watching a *mysterious* movie,
In this movie, I can't forward or
Rewind the scenes,
And i can't skip any part in the movie,
I have to watch the whole movie with conscious,
Each and every second increases my curious,
And I'm biting my nail and waiting,
What is going to happen next?
And i don't know where the "end" is going to be in the
movie,
I have never seen the interesting movie
Like this,
The movie name is "life",
Which is directed by " god".

50. Natural Shower

I love the way, your tiny droplets
touches my *cheeks*,
In that moment my worries are getting *weak*,
I can hear your sounds of *sizzling*,
And my wounds are getting cure
By your *drizzling*,
I can know about your arrival by *petrichor*,
And that my most favourite *flavour*,
Your beautiful *fragrance*
Makes me to *dance*,
Yeah that's you, "my natural shower",
You're helping bestie to farmer.

51. Best Companion

In my childhood days, I felt *lonely*,
At that time, god gave me a precious
Gift called *sisterly*,
Where she came to share my parental *love*,
That minute, it gave me a hardest *move*,
But some years later, she always scoring
High by caring me,
Sometimes i feel jealous of her,
How she can fabulous acts,
Her cute smile makes me to immobile,
And you can face the problems like *monster*,
When you're having like this lovely *sister*.

52. Story of My Room

Sometimes I want to be in a *dark room*,
That place may be my *bedroom*,
Now I'm lying on a white cotton of *bed*,
Which it gives dreams as a carpet in the
Colour of *pale red*,
And I hug my rosy *pillows*,
That second, I lost my fussy *sorrows*,
Now I'm in the moderate *temperature*,
Because it's the shadow of *nature*,
Finally, I closed my eyes *without sleep*,
And I don't know how that *deep*?
Then I wake up with a refreshment,
And it should be an unforgettable moment.

53.First Touch

When I opened my eyes, I saw a beautiful face,
Where he kept me in his strong hands, I felt like in palace,
He laughed at me while
I made childish acts,
He is the one who trust me without any distract,
He never allows me to cry,
That's why my eyes are always dry,
Many times, I exclaimed, how can he show more caring
and affection,
And he gives more freedom without any restriction,
His happiness in my happiness,
So, he always makes me to feel loveliness,
Now I want to tell frankly, he is my first love and he is my
last love,
Where I can't move, until I have to prove.

54.Single Key

Love has no spare keys,
It has only *one key* which is original,
If you lose it, you can't
Find it back,
So, keep it *safe*.

55. Brain vs Heart

Don't let your brain control your *heart*,
Coz brain always think about the temporary happiness,
Heart always thinks about the *permanent happiness.*

56. Beauty of Nature

Sometimes I can't escape from the beauty of skyscape,
While it's glittering in reddish orange with chill wind,
It became an indelible image in my mind,
It spreads the reflections,
and which conveys its information,
When it changes from day to night,
And I'm watching the unbelievable sight,
It can easily change my bad mood,
Because it has the nature of motherhood,
No words to express,
Only then I know it's another way to impress,
Thus, god's creativity breaks all the negativity.

57. Who you are?

Ask yourself, why we are living in this world?
And our life looks like a battlefield,
We're fighting for something with others in the war,
Because we want to be in shining star,
But we don't know, how to achieve our goal,

And it should not be done by some magical,
Don't be a gold fish in little fish tank,
Be a diano fish in large sea sink,
You've to choose your depth in your life,
That makes you live in a super safe.

58.Stress Buster

Whenever I get depressed, I love to be sit alone in terrace,
Where I saw the moon and some stars were surrounded
me in the cool surface,
Instantly, some bright light, it attracts me towards it,
Now I'm watching the brightest star
Which is twinkling in the moonlight,
And I feel the breezy moment with cool star,
And it's want to tell something to me, but I can't hear it,
coz it's too far,
Every night I'm watching the distinctive star,
It's never leave me, because it's my
Ever favourite elegant star.

59.Be Expressive

Being normal is boring to me,
It's like an artificial to me,
Where I'm searching the natural,
Which gives me the original,
Never be the unreal to the real,

If you're loyal to yourself,
You will have the royal in yourself,
Start the initial with ideal,
Then it reveals the best final,
Be special to others,
And share the moral,
But never forget to be jovial.

60.Know your Value

Your presence should give the happiness to others,
But your absence should give the emptiness to others,
When you are *satisfied* with this one, you're leading a very good life,
And never use the words which are very sharp like knife,
Keep far away from the loved one,
Then only, they can know the *precious* value of you,
Until keep calm and enjoy the *beauty* of life.

61.Social Media survives, Life Dies

By using Instagram, even we can't get the milligram of happiness,
From Facebook, we can't face our parents in day to day life,
On Twitter, we can't listen the *tweets* of birds,
From the Snapchat, we can't chat with neighbours,

Finally, by using WhatsApp, really, we don't know?
What's going in your home?
Social media pauses all our life of inertia,
It's just an entertainment not an achievement,
You can say i'm just watching these all for some time,
But you're really wasting your *valuable* lifetime.

62. Don't use Her

Never treat a woman like a slave,
Because she is the one who can give a lot of love,
Never see her through a lust,
And never blow her like a dust,
If you use her as a thing,
She will smash you with her *fire of wing*,
Never spread rumours about an innocent woman,
I don't request you to be like a superhuman,
I just want you to be like a human.

63. Life for Love

It's like a ball, it will bounce back to you,
It's like a wave, it will always come towards you,
It's like a shadow, it will always come with you,
It's like a moon, it's always follow you,
It's like some stars, because it's uncountable and
unlimited,

It's like a book, it always disturbs you to read and
increases your curiosity,
And it reveals you, it's a four-letter magic,
It will bring you, and it's called "love"

64. Longing for Love

Whenever you're hugged by your
Mom and dad,
Just think about
Orphanage children,
So always be *grateful* to your
Mom and dad.

65. Fake Dinner

Many people don't have
The dinner to eat, but many people
Forget their dinner to get the title of
"winner winner chicken dinner".

66. Color of Heart

Let's keep
Your heart as white,
Without any *dirt*.

67.Theory of Life

The world is a *temporary* one,
Then how can you think that people
Only permanent?
Everything has to change,
That's the life.

68.Neglect Negativity

Don't bother about people,
Sometimes they praise you,
Sometimes they curse you,
So, *ignore* them.

69.Fame your Name

Let's this world
Know your name
By your *fame*.

70.Success is Yours

Fight against your
Fear, because
Success is near.

71.Something special in you

Try to find something new
In yourself, assume your
Talents are few,
You've to be *renew*.

72.Love Matters

Write beyond letters,
Think beyond imagination,
Love beyond life.

73.Strength of Smile

If someone hurt you
Means, slap them with your
Cutest smile.

74.Painful Punishment

The best punishment
To your enemy is,
Forgive them.

75.Own your Success

Your success begins, when
You're *encouraging* others success,
It becomes your success.

76.Stop Stalking

If you don't know
About others means,
Let's *feel happy*,
Coz you're living your life.

77.Let's Open Up

Everyone is gifted,
But many people never
Try to *open* it.

78.Real Happiness

Real happiness is, being
A stepping stones
To *others success*.

79.My Rain Diary

Rain is an *unmeasurable* gain,
Which heals every
Farmer's pain.

80.Shade of Pure Heart

Never see the colour of the skin,
See the colour of the *heart*.

81.Deep Truth

Many times, words are "pain killer",
But sometimes words are
" pain" and "killer".

82. Listen to the Heart

See your *beauty* not by mirror,
It may show error,
See by your *heart*.

83. Is love wins?

Love is like a balloon,
If it filled with *lust* means,
It will burst.

84. Pure is Sure

Pure love *cures* everything,
But fake love breaks everything.

85. Endless Relationship

Online friendship is,
Two hearts are
Always *connected* even in
An offline.

86. Distract Destroys you

Stop focusing on the waste things
Which distracts you,
Do the best things which *attracts*
Everyone to you.

87. First Love

There is only one relationship,
Whatever you hate or hurt it,
It doesn't consider that,
Instead of it,
It loves you blindly,
I wondered!
How can it possible?
The *indefinable relationship* is called
"mom's love".

88.Be good at Heart

Royalty comes from your *behaviour*,
Loyalty comes from your heart.

89.Key Point of Relationship

Relationship is like a question and answer,
If you can't "understand" the questions means,
You can't answer it,
"understanding" plays a vital role
in all relationship.

90.Fall in Goal

Your goal may *long* to reach,
Don't bother about it,
Because it never be wrong.

91.Pain Healer

If you give respect to her feeling
Surely, she will cure your wounds by healing,
Coz it's not a pressure to her,
It's a *pleasure* to her.

92.Non-stop Beating

Dear heart,
How can you *accept*
This all hurting's?
But still beating?

93.Trust me First

The best moments,
Will *happen* after
The worst moments.

94.Mark my Words

If someone trust you blindly,
Without any hesitation,
Never *misuse* them or
Never use them.

95.Loss of Life

Loss of care leads to loss of love,
Loss of love leads to loss of happiness,
Loss of happiness leads to loss of life.

96.Feel from Heart

If you want to
Close to someone,
First *understand*
Their feelings.

97.Mixture of Life

Life is a *mixture* of bitter sweet moments,
So always remember the sweet moments.

98.Super Power

Everyone having a super power,
Is nothing but your *self-confidence*.

99.Zero to Infinity

Never fix any "limit" in your relationship,
It leads to "split".

100.Never Quit

It's better to be *quiet* than
Quit the relationship.

101.Life Mate

Love is not about
Finding a life partner,
Love is all about
Understanding a life partner.

102.Imperfection

First check yourself before
Advice others,
If you're perfect
You can proceed.

103.Never Give Up

Life laughs on
You, when
You accept the
Failure.

104.Love isn't a Theorem

If you have to
Prove your love
To someone,
It's not a love.

105.Black Beauty

I look at the velvety blackness
Of the sky,
And i see the wonders of god's magic,
Still *stunned* and freezed
About the dark nature.

106. Expect the Unexpected

When things don't go as expected,
Just *keep calm*,
Coz expected things
Never happen in expected time,
It's only happen in unexpected time.

107. Worthable Wait

Precious things won't
Come easily,
It *takes time*.

108. Be Strong

In every week, we're getting
Weak by thinking of
Our past, so *forget*
It fast.

109. Life's Truth

Everything happens for
A valid *reason*,
So, accept it.

110. Shadow of You

Pure love may
Makes you
Wait, but never
Ever leave you.

111. Reflection of Love

True love does not come
By an attraction, it's only
Comes by an *affection*.

112.Adorable Arrival

Recover soon from your past,
Coz wonderful future is *waiting*
For your arrival.

113.Nature kills Torture

The one and only way to
Escape from life's torture is,
Spend your time with nature.

114.Life Style

Design your life as
Whatever you want,
But don't forget
To *implement* it.

115. Current Situation

People never changes, but
Situation changes everyone in
their life.

116. Happy Life

If you want to lead a
Happy life, then you have to
Delete some people in
Your life.

117. Light at Night

The night whispers to me,
I'm not dark,
I'm the reason for
Tomorrow's spark.

118. Whose Life?

Never live your life for
Others wish,
Live your life for
Your wish,
Coz it's not others life,
It's *yours*.

119. Lifeline

Life is like a game,
Whenever you made a mistake,
It always offers you a *lifeline*.

120. Unconditional Love

Caring someone unconditionally
Is not a big deal,
But, will it
Last forever?

121. Disability isn't an Inability

Moon too has
A stain in it,
But *still bright*.

122. Inner Voice

When there is no life
To live,
But some inner voice
Helps to lead your life,
That's called *hope*.

123. Role of Every soul

A mother is not about to
Cook and clean the home,
She is about to love us and
Guide us to reach the fame.

124.Success formula

Persistence + patience = success
Persistence and patience are the
Two eyes of success,
If you lose one,
You can't get the
Clear vision of success.

125.Slogan of Life

Be honest,
Ignore the worst,
Keep the trust,
Then, you're the *best*.

126.Unlucky People

Never feel about the people
Those who leave you,
Coz they're not eligible to
Come with you to your entire life
And *share* your success.

127. Time of Love

True love will arrive you,
When you're having a *pure heart*.

128. Ego kills

If there is an "ego" in your
Relationship,
You can't "go"
Through a successful life.

129. Beauty of Love

If you see the beauty through eyes
It's called *lust*,
If you see the beauty through heart
It's called *love*.

130.Find the Fake

You can find the fake people,
In your success, they will be *with* you,
But in your failure, they will *leave* you.

131.You're Unique

Never expect that everyone
Should love you,
Coz not everyone has the ability
To *understand* you.

132.Success Date

Life may be going through your fate,
But that fate too has your success date.

133.Sign of Success

Be a solution to someone's problem,
Be a reason to someone's success,
Be a smile in someone's lip,
Be a soul in someone's body,
Be a love in someone's life,
Be a beat in someone's heart.

134.Individuality

Don't be in a group like shepherd,
It's difficult to find you,
Stand away from it,
Then everyone can easily identify and see you.

135.Life Aspects

Ask yourself, what was the purpose I created?
Keep the good people around you,
Let's go through the path to *achieve* your destiny.

136. Move on

Slowly, one step at a time,
When you're *frequently* walk in
One step by step,
Surely, you'll reach your goal
Coz you're *moving*.

137. Book of the Year

God gave us an expensive book,
It has 24 chapters,
And it consists of 365 pages,
These pages consist of 86400 letters,
Whenever you turn over the page,
You can learn lessons from each page,
Speciality of the book is,
You can read the book only one time in your life time,
And you can't read backward,
The book is awesome and interesting
Those whose who read
in an optimistic way,
The book is worst and boring those who
Read in a pessimistic way,
So, try to complete the book in
best manner,
Coz another amazing book is waiting for you,
The book's edition of the year is "2020".

138.Life's Secret

Life is like a magnet,
Whatever you want to attract
It can attract towards you
You're the responsibility of your life,
So, *attract* good things only,
And *repel* the bad things.

139.Life Spoiler

Three letters word " lie" in a relationship,
Which leads to die.

140.Focus on Future

Past is waste,
Future is torture,
But present is predominant,
So, don't waste your precious time about past,
Never ruin yourself with torture of
Over thinking about future,
So, *focus* on the present,
And make your life as predominant.

141. Worryless Heart

Maturity fails in front of childishness,
So be like a *child* without worries.

142. Expectations Hurts

If you *hate* the expectations,
Expectations will never hurt you.

143. Feel Better

Whenever life pulls you to
The hardest moment,
Take a long breath
And just say,
This too shall *pass*.

144. Beautify your Life

Life is unbeautiful,
Until you love yourself
Life is unsuccessful,
Until you know yourself.

145. Higher Humanity

If you want to increase
Your humanity,
Then give charity.

146. Meaningless Life

Life is nothing
Without thrilling,
Life is nonsense
Without suspense,
Life is foul
Without goal.

147.Life Begins

Never live in a comfort zone,
It will *dump* you under the
Sand like a little stone.

148.Satisfaction Speaks

Insufficient storage in my heart
For expectations,
Coz my heart is filled with *satisfaction*.

149.Wondering the World

I exclaimed how beautiful
These stars are!
It never stops twinkling,
I exclaimed how beautiful
These birds are!
It's never stops singing and migrating,
I exclaimed how beautiful
This world is!
It's never stops it's revolving,
I exclaimed how beautiful
we are!
We're the best one in god's creations
Why we only stop our work
And lose hope for
Our silly problems?

150. Destiny of Success

Hard work is the,
Landmark of success.

151. Best Planer of All

Sometimes things don't go as
Planned,
So never worry about it,
But remember one thing,
All things are going perfectly
In *god's plan*.

152. Unmeasurable

Love is like an ocean,
You can't measure the *depth* of it.

153. Peaceful Life

If you want to get the *best things*
Means, just "forget" the worst things,
If you want to give the best one to others
Means, just "forgive" the worst one.

154. What is Love?

When one heart is longing for a
Care is called love,
If someone is hungry for a long time,
When you give them food
By your caring heart,
It's also called love.

155. Success Love Poem

Love means never having to
Outer looks and lust,
But it's having about a
Inner look and trust.

156.Speech of Self-Motivation

Don't wait for someone to
Encourage you or *motivate* you,
If you wait for it,
You can't achieve,
So, write this in your mind,
I never stop *working*,
And I should blow like a wind.

157.Melting Moon

The moon stares at me,
Coz nowadays, many of us
Not watching the *moonlight*,
Instead of it, we're
Watching the *phone light*.

158.Need of World

The world doesn't need
Your hard work,
It needs your result only
So, work hardly to attain
The best *results*.

159.Origin of Love

Trust is the origin of love,
Don't test and doubt the trust on love,
Because it's very *sensitive*,
And it's very painful to those
Who are *additive* on love.

160.Familiour Name

One day, this world will
Know your *name* through your fame,
But think about it,
When will it call you?
And what are the steps you're doing
Now to gain the fame?

161.Thoughts become Facts

Life is like a bucket,
Ego is like a hole,
Love is like a water,
If there is a hole,
Your love will leak and
It will dry your life,
Then your life will
Become empty.

162.Precious Gift Ever

You will love the nature,
When you realize,
that's your future.

163.Raise your Voice

You're not a dump okay?
Just speak out, what do you
Want to be?
Never burn your
Dreams for anyone
Coz it's not others life,
It's your life.

164.Universal Language

Smile speaks beautiful
Language than silence,
Just keep moving with
Smile across the *life's mile*.

165.False Solution

Life is not about to die
For a silly reason,
Life is about to live and
To knows your *birth's reason*.

166.Recipe of Life

Let's make a *tastiest recipe*
Of your life by adding
Happiness, positive thoughts,
Helping mind, kind words and
Caring love.

167.Grab the Gold

Every day, you're getting an *opportunity*,
If you can grab it, then you can create your own identity.

168. Good Time Vs Bad Time

Good time is, when you
Use it perfectly,
Bad time is, when you waste
It perfectly.

169. Beauty of Relationship

We can't see the beautiful
Twinkling of stars without *night*,
Like that, we can't understand our
Loved one without any *fight*.

170. Wrong Sight

Never judge others *wrongly*
By listening others words,
And there is no use after
Losing them.

171.Journey of Life

My life is going on like a bike ride,
It's smooth and little tough
With speed breaks,
And many road rules as *life rules*,
I've to wait and obey the traffic rules to
Reach my destiny,
I thoroughly *enjoying* my travel,
And I don't know,
Where my vehicle fuel will end.

172.Amazing Tool

Nature is an amazing tool
To restart your life machine,
It paves a *pleasant journey*.

173.Don't be statue

When things are not moving,
But you should keep moving,
Coz in this busy world,
If you're not *move*,
Even little ant will eat you.

174. Wrong Answer

You're like a wrong answer,
But many people thought,
It gives a permanent solution,
Yup, it's a *suicide*,
Actually, it's not a solution,
It's a *destruction*.

175. Journey of Success

Success is not a *station* to
Reach it,
It's a *journey* to travel in it.

176. Light of Life

Hope is like a torch,
When you fall in dark,
It will *help* you to reach
The place where you want.

177. Two kinds of People

There are two kinds of people,
Some people lives in
Our memories as *real*,
Some people lives in reality
As *reel*.

178. Life Message

If there's one truth I learnt by living
This life of mine,
It is this,
Whatever the bad situation you have,
Just keep *patience* with you,
Coz patience will *change*
the situation as well.

179. Magic of Life

Life is also a magic,
Where it gives
Some *unpredictable* things,
And it also takes an
Unbelievable things.

180. You're the Best

Don't feel
That you're not loved
By anyone,
Just *love yourself.*

181. Life Molder

Books are like a
Character *molding tool,*
If you read it one time,
It will motivate you to be
A right man,
If you open it,
You never want to close it,
That's the *magic* of book.

182. Learn to be Peace

Life is best lived when
You learn to *segregate* the
Good people and bad people
In your life.

183. Definition of Time

Time is precious
When you want to own it,
Time is free
When you don't need it,
Time is your friend
When you're in a happy mode,
Time is your foe
When you're in a bad mood,
So, time is in your hand to
Change what is good for you.

184. Why can't you?

Anytime we can receive the call
From death,
So, lead your life in a faith path,
We don't know when we will go,
In this small life, why can't you
Give up your *ego*.

185. Feel the Feelings

Try to give respect
To others feelings,
Coz it's hurt, when
You're *ignoring* by others.

186.Do you Remember it?

Don't say,
My life moves like
A *tortoise*,
Remember the
Familiar childhood story.

187.Unvaluable one

Don't feel that no one
Knows your value,
You're not gold to know
About your value,
Yes, you're *precious*,
You're *beyond* that those
Valuable things

188.Easy Learning

Life lessons are harder
When you didn't learn from it,
Life lessons are very simpler,
When you try to *understand* it.

189. Perfection of Success

If persistence gives perfection means,
Then *patience* gives success.

190. Composition of Love

Love is like a piano
Whatever you *play*,
It always gives out music,
Few music become popular,
Others become failure,
Everything in your way of playing.

191. Lesson from Blossoms

Flowers make me believe that
it will wither at end of the day,
But it never stops spreading its fragrance,
Likewise, you never lose the *hope*
Until your end.

192.Dreams are Awaken

Your dreams are getting awake,
When you're sacrificing your sleep.

193.Philosophy of Love

In the beginning, love seems like a
Little pond with *small depth*,
Years later, love turns out to be
Like a largest sea which has *no depth*.

194.Phonoholic

Never *type*,
While you're speaking
Or listening to your parents.

195. Humanity Left

Everywhere machine and
Animals in the world,
One is *working* with effort,
Another is *hunting* without heart.

196. Uncover the Brain

Cover the book
By *uncovering* it's deep meaning of
Every word,
And cover the ignorance by
Uncovering the *knowledge* of books.

197. Colourful life

Nothing can quench your thirst
Then *water*,
It has no colour,
But it's the reason of the
Colour of rainbow,
If you save the water,
It will give you a colourful life.

198.Fear Fails

Don't run
When facing the fear,
Face it,
Face to face in near.

199.Find out

Don't blame
Others that they don't
Have *humanity*,
First find out from you.

200.How do I tell you?

I don't know
What it is?
I don't know
Where it is?
Then only I know
It's a *feel*.

You can contact the Publisher at:
www.fanatixx.in